BERA THE ONE-HEADED TROLL

Eric Orchard

:01

First Second
New York

For my mother

First Second

Copyright © 2016 by Eric Orchard
Published by First Second
First Second is an imprint of Roaring Brook Press,
a division of Holtzbrinck Publishing Holdings Limited Partnership
175 Fifth Avenue, New York, New York 10010
All rights reserved

Library of Congress Control Number: 2015944380

ISBN: 978-1-62672-106-7

Our books may be purchased in bulk for promotional, educational, or business use. Please
contact your local bookseller or the Macmillan Corporate and Premium Sales Department at
(800) 221-7945 ext. 5442 or by e-mail at MacmillanSpecialMarkets@macmillan.com.

With special thanks to Andrew Arnold

FIRST
EDITION

First edition 2016
Book design by Gordon Whiteside
Printed in China by RR Donnelley Asia Printing Solutions Ltd, Dongguan City, Guangdong Province
1 3 5 7 9 10 8 6 4 2

BY ART
WE LIVE

SOMEWHERE NORTH AND EAST THERE IS A SECRET COVE. AND IN THAT COVE IS A TINY ISLAND. AND ON THAT ISLAND LIVED A SMALL TROLL WITH ONE HEAD.

WINSLOWE, CAN YOU MOVE THE CANDLE OVER THIS WAY?

THE SMALL, ONE-HEADED TROLL WAS THE OFFICIAL PUMPKIN GARDENER OF THE TROLL KING.

THE PUMPKINS ARE SO BIG THIS YEAR, BERA! YOU MUST BE THE BEST GARDENER EVER.

I JUST HAVE GOOD SOIL AND FAIR WEATHER!

BUT THERE ARE NO KINGS OR QUEENS IN THIS STORY.

SORRY, WINSLOWE. I'M ASKING MY AUNT'S GHOST. SHE KNOWS A LOT.

OKAY, BUT DON'T EXPECT HER TO MAKE SENSE.

POP

BERA! MY FAVORITE NIECE!

OH! WHERE DID YOU GET A BABY?

WE FOUND IT OUTSIDE. I THINK IT'S HUNGRY.

GOO?

14

15

THE FORCE AT THE DOOR IS MALIGNANT AND EVIL!

IT IS?

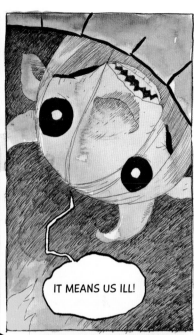

IT MEANS US ILL!

MAYBE WE'D BETTER HIDE THE BABY.

SH-SHOULD I GET MY SWORD?

NO! IT WON'T DO ANY GOOD!

KNOCK KNOCK!

19

CRASH

THEY MAKE THE BEST MINDLESS MONSTERS! JUST THROW THEM IN A VAT WITH CERTAIN ELIXIRS, AND...

BOOM! INSTANT MONSTER!

UH... WOW...

WOW, INDEED! I'M HOPING THE KING WILL BE SUITABLY IMPRESSED.

I THINK PRESENTING THE KING WITH A NEW MONSTER WILL EARN ME A PLACE IN THE COURT AGAIN.

WELL. I'D BEST BE OFF. THAT LITTLE CREATURE WON'T COOK UP ITSELF.

OH DEAR.

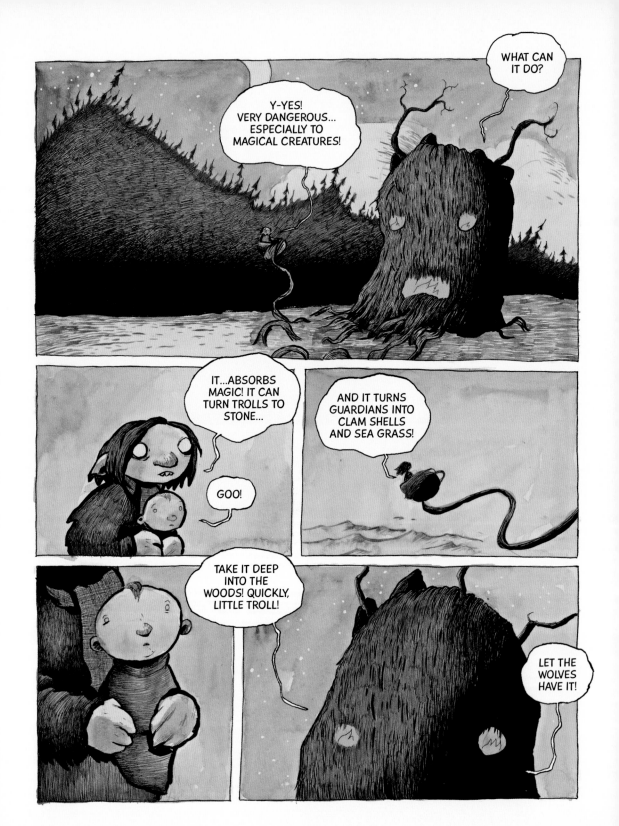

34

38

40

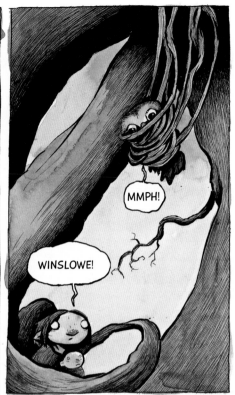

41

43

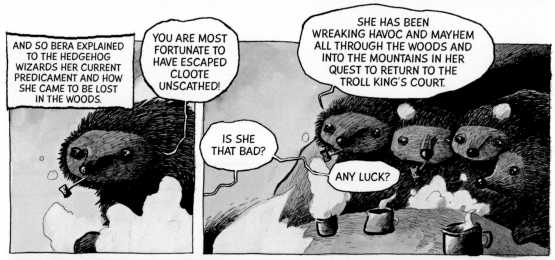

45

46

DO I KNOCK?

I'VE NEVER VISITED ANYONE BEFORE.

THE HEDGEHOGS ARE GONE...

HUFF, HUFF

HURRY, BERA! I CAN SEE THE SUN!

HEY, IS THAT A BABY?

YES, IT'S A HUMAN BABY, MR. WULF.

WELL, LOOK AT THAT. HOW DID YOU GET YOURSELF A HUMAN BABY?

I FOUND IT, SIR.

GAH.

IMAGINE THAT! WHO DID YOU SAY YOU WERE AGAIN?

I DIDN'T, SIR. I'M BERA, THE PUMPKIN GARDENER.

I DON'T REMEMBER ASKING FOR A GARDENER...

I NEED A HERO, SIR. I WAS HOPING YOU COULD RETURN THE BABY TO THE HUMANS.

WHY DON'T YOU DO IT, BARREL?

...

ME??? HA HA HA!

I'M JUST A PUMPKIN GARDENER, SIR.

YES, IT WAS SMART TO COME TO ME. I AM A GREAT WARRIOR. I WILL HELP YOU.

OH, SLEEPING MOSTLY.

I HAD BEEN SLEEPING FOR TWENTY YEARS WHEN YOU WOKE ME UP.

HMM... WHAT WERE WE TALKING ABOUT?

SLEEPING?

OH! YOU'RE SLEEPY? YOU CAN HAVE THE BEDROOM AT THE TOP OF THE STAIRS.

56

57

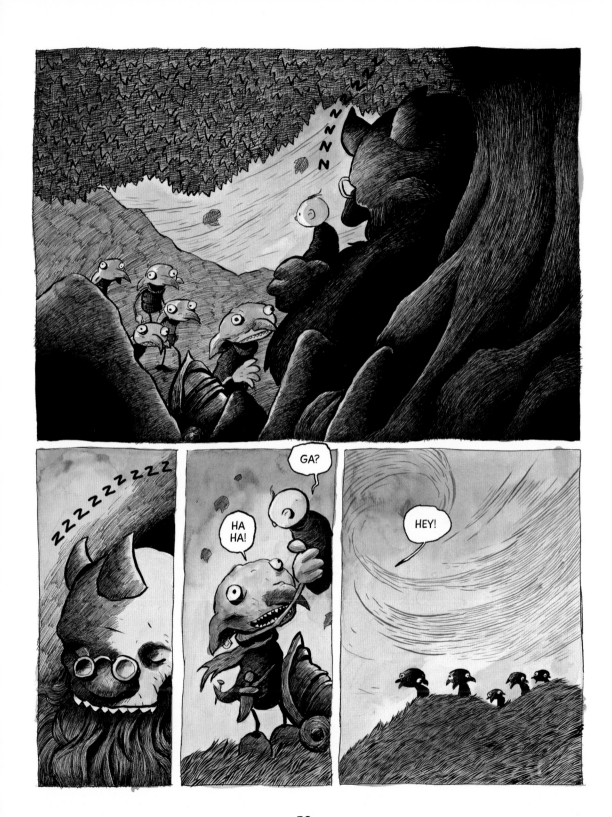

AND SO BERA PUSHED ON. FOR THREE NIGHTS SHE TRAVELED, SPENDING HER DAYS IN CAVES AND HOLES.

SOON SHE FOUND HERSELF VERY, VERY LOST.

WINSLOWE FLEW AHEAD, LOOKING FOR A FAMILIAR TREE OR ROCK OR STREAM. BUT EVERYTHING WAS STRANGE TO BOTH OF THEM.

UNTIL THEY CAME TO A SWAMP THAT SPRAWLED IN ALL DIRECTIONS.

THIS IS STAR MURK SWAMP! LOOK! IT'S IN MY BOOK!

SO WE SHOULD TURN BACK, RIGHT?

NO, LOOK! DUKE OTIG LIVES HERE! ONE OF THE HEROES OF THE TROLL-GIANT WAR!

HE LIVES IN A GIANT TREE IN THE MIDDLE OF THE SWAMP.

WHAT'S HE LIKE?

I'M NOT SURE. THERE AREN'T MANY STORIES ABOUT HIM.

64

71

SIP

LOOK OUT, SIR! IT'S CLOOTE'S SPIES!

SPIES?

THAT'S HARSH!

IT WAS THESE FINE CREATURES WHO HELPED ME MAKE THE SLEEPING POTION YOU'RE DRINKING.

GAK!

YOU'RE WORKING FOR CLOOTE!

WITH CLOOTE!

OTIG WORKS ONLY FOR HIMSELF!

THERE'S A PASSAGE BACK THERE!

GRRRR

GRRRRR

CAN YOU SQUEEZE THROUGH?

BARELY. TOO MANY PUMPKIN TARTS, I GUESS.

WHERE ARE WE?

IT'S THE OLD KITCHEN.

AS THE TREE KEEPS GROWING, LOTS OF ROOMS GET ABANDONED.

LISTEN.

SOMEONE'S COMING.

WHO'S THERE?

PFFT! I BET IT'S THOSE RATS AGAIN.

82

HEY! YOU'RE NOT A GOBLIN AT ALL!

NO, I—

HISS!

GET HER!

GRRR!

OTIG'S GONNA KILL US!

OH GEEZ!

UMM...

THIS IS BAD.

86

SPLAT

CLIK CLAK CLIK

THAT SOUND!

OH NO!

BERA RAN BLINDLY THROUGH THE SWAMP. IT WOVE NASTY MAGICS TO CONFOUND HER, AND SHE BECAME MORE LOST THAN SHE'D EVER BEEN.

STRANGE VOICES ECHOED THROUGH THE FOG AND MIST, TRYING TO LEAD BERA INTO SINKING PITS OR OVER CLIFFS. BUT SHE IGNORED THEM AND PUSHED ON.

SHE AVOIDED THE STRANGE, DANGEROUS CREATURES OF THE SWAMP UNTIL...

...SHE STUMBLED ON SOME HUNGRY SHADOW WOLVES.

THOSE WOLVES AREN'T LOOKING FOR ME!

THEY WANT THAT POOR GOBLIN.

HE DOESN'T HAVE LONG. I'D BETTER DO SOMETHING.

I'M GETTING SICK OF TREES.

GOBLIN! UP HERE!

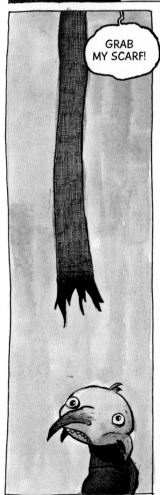

I HOPE THIS MEANS THINGS ARE GOING TO GET BETTER.

BUT WITH MY LUCK, YOU NEVER KNOW.

BERA!

WE HEARD YOU WERE CAPTURED. WE RUSHED TO FIND YOU.

HOW DID YOU FIND ME? THIS SWAMP IS SO CONFUSING!

THE RATS!

WE'RE THE ONLY CREATURES WHO CAN NAVIGATE THE SWAMP BESIDES OTIG!

BUT WE CAN CATCH UP WHILE WE WALK.

CLOOTE IS SEARCHING FOR YOU IN HER BOAT! IT'S ONLY A MATTER OF TIME BEFORE SHE FINDS YOU.

VINCE LED THE FRIENDS OUT OF THE TORTUOUS SWAMP AND UP INTO THE HILLS BEYOND.

DOES ANYONE HAVE ANY IDEA WHERE WE ARE?

AH! CLOOTE'S SPIES!

i. CRUNCH!

GET THEM ALL!

NO! KEEP GOING!

I'M NOT DEAD.

H-HELLO?
NANNA?

UP HERE,
FRIEND.

AWK!

I WILL HAVE THE BABY NOW.

DON'T FRET, BERA.

THAT BABY HAS NO FAMILY.

THEY ARE ALL DEAD. IT IS UNLOVED, AND NOT A SOUL WILL MISS IT.

NO!

THE JOURNEY HOME FROM THE EDGE OF THE TROLL KINGDOM WAS MUCH LESS EVENTFUL.

BERA'S ISLAND LOOKED SMALLER TO HER NOW.

BUT AT THAT MOMENT, THE LITTLE ISLAND WAS THE MOST BEAUTIFUL THING BERA HAD EVER SEEN.

THE WHEEL OF SEASONS TURNED, AND ONCE MORE IT WAS TIME FOR BERA TO HARVEST HER PUMPKINS.

THESE MUST BE THE BIGGEST PUMPKINS EVER, BERA!